NiBBLES O'HARE

BETTY PARASKEVAS

MICHAEL PARASKEVAS

SIMON & SCHUSTER BOOKS FOR YOUNG READERS

New York   London   Toronto   Sydney   Singapore

Nibbles O'Hare lived
in an underground apartment
in the heart of Lincoln Park. It
was elegantly furnished with
treasures he had rescued
from the trash around town.

Every morning Nibbles tiptoed into the kitchen of the park's fancy restaurant. He would fill his shopping basket with the most tender carrots and perfect lettuce leaves.

He always welcomed an interruption by one of the chefs, because he loved the chase that was sure to follow.

But the owner of the restaurant became angry and tacked up a WANTED poster with a picture of Nibbles. Nibbles agreed with his best friend, Struts, to leave the city. They made their escape in the back of a vegetable truck.

As the truck raced away, a strong gust of wind ripped the poster from the tree and sent it skipping along the street.

When the truck finally stopped, Nibbles and Struts got out. After a while they came to an abandoned mansion. And in the woods surrounding it they found a child's playhouse in disrepair.

"I was thinking, Struts," he began.

"Please don't think, Nibbles," Struts pleaded. "We're in enough trouble. It's dangerous when you think."

"But we can fix this place up— soap and water, a fresh coat of paint . . . ," he replied.

At that moment a squirrel dropped out of a tree. "Allow me to introduce myself. I'm Wacky Shellhammer, at your service. Come on! Come on! I'll show you around."

Nibbles and Struts fixed the roof, painted the tiny house inside and out, and polished the windows till they sparkled.

Wacky Shellhammer busied himself sewing curtains and bed linens.

At last the house was finished. As the weary trio ate dinner that night, Nibbles and Struts invited Wacky to move in. The little fellow was beside himself with joy, and they all slept well, snuggled under their new quilts.

But the next morning they were awakened by a group of enraged rabbits.

"You have no right to this fine house," yelled one rabbit.

"Clear out," cried another.

Struts wondered what scheme Nibbles would pull out of his hat.

Nibbles raised his hand for silence. When he finally spoke, his voice was like rolling thunder: "Return to your homes and leave me in peace, because—because— I am the EASTER BUNNY!"

Wacky gushed, "I knew you had to be somebody important, but gee, the Easter Bunny!"

"I tell you, he's a fraud," insisted a rabbit called One-Eyed Jack, but the others had fallen under the spell of Nibbles O'Hare.

The rivers began to swell with melting snow and the days were growing longer. Once again a group of rabbits gathered in front of the little house.

"Sir," said a spokesrabbit, "the Easter season will soon be here. Tell us what we can do to help."

Nibbles had almost forgotten that he had claimed to be the Easter Bunny, but he replied calmly, "I was just about to call for volunteers."

In the weeks that followed, the rabbits worked feverishly. Candy headquarters was established in the kitchen of the mansion.

Not everything went smoothly. The rabbits did a magnificent job of dyeing the eggs. However, they forgot to boil them first, and the whole job had to be done over.

Wacky Shellhammer fashioned a proper Easter Rabbit outfit for Nibbles, and finally the big night arrived.

The rabbits waited in line for Wacky and Struts to fill their Easter baskets, then reported to Nibbles, who plotted their delivery routes on a huge map.

Meanwhile, One-Eyed Jack found an old poster lying on the side of the road.

"I knew it," he snapped, and he hurried off to show it to the rabbits.

When they saw the poster, the rabbits were furious. "I told you he was a fraud," boasted Jack.

The poster that had hung in Lincoln Park had miraculously caught up with Nibbles after all this time.

"Make your own deliveries!" the rabbits shouted.

"All right," Nibbles admitted, "I'm not the Easter Bunny, but if you'll help me, I promise I'll leave tomorrow."

Wacky tried to reason with them, but the rabbits began to walk away.

"I guess I'll have to do the job myself," murmured Nibbles.

He strapped on a delivery basket and took off on his first run. Wacky and Struts stood by, ready to reload. And then it began to rain.

The rabbits watched as Nibbles returned again and again, his lovely suit soaked, his ears drooping. When he slipped in the mud they laughed.

With each hour that passed, the rain fell harder. Wacky and Struts pleaded with Nibbles to give up.

Nibbles was showing signs of fatigue. Once again he slipped in the mud, but this time the rabbits didn't laugh.

It was almost dawn and still raining when Nibbles heard Struts say, "You did it, fella."

Nibbles smiled and collapsed.

The rabbits, impressed with his courage, rushed to help, but Wacky snapped, "We'll manage, thank you very much!" He and Struts carried Nibbles into the tiny house and slammed the door.

Wacky and Struts spoon-fed Nibbles hot carrot soup and never left his side as he slept all day and straight through the next night. The following morning Nibbles rose, still a bit shaky, and said, "Well, Struts, I guess it's time to be on our way."

"First," said Wacky, "there are some rabbits waiting to see you."

Nibbles stepped outside and was greeted with a rousing cheer led by One-Eyed Jack. "The rabbits want you to stay, Nibbles," he said, "and—well, so do I."

"Yippee," cried Wacky.

SIMON & SCHUSTER BOOKS FOR YOUNG READERS
An imprint of Simon & Schuster Children's Publishing Division
1230 Avenue of the Americas, New York, New York 10020
Text copyright © 2001 by Rita E. Paraskevas
Illustrations copyright © 2001 by Michael P. Paraskevas

Book design by Jennifer Reyes
The text of this book is set in Centennial.
The illustrations are rendered in acrylic on paper.
Printed in Hong Kong
10 9 8 7 6 5 4 3 2 1

Library of Congress Cataloging-in-Publication Data

Paraskevas, Betty.
Nibbles O'Hare / by Betty Paraskevas ; illustrated by Michael Paraskevas.
  p. cm.
Summary: Having moved to the country and convinced his new neighbors that he is
the Easter Bunny, Nibbles O'Hare finds himself forced to carry out the duty of deliver-
ing a multitude of Easter baskets.
ISBN 0-689-82865-9
[1. Rabbits Fiction. 2. Easter Fiction.] I. Paraskevas, Michael, 1961- ill. II. Title.
PZ7.P2135Ni 2001
[E]—dc21
99-31242

To our editor, David Gale,
for his guidance and sound
advice

first
edition

And so, Nibbles and Struts stayed, and somewhere, deep in the woods, there's a tiny house with a sign above the door that reads:

This is the *home of* Nibbles O'Hare, our Easter Bunny.